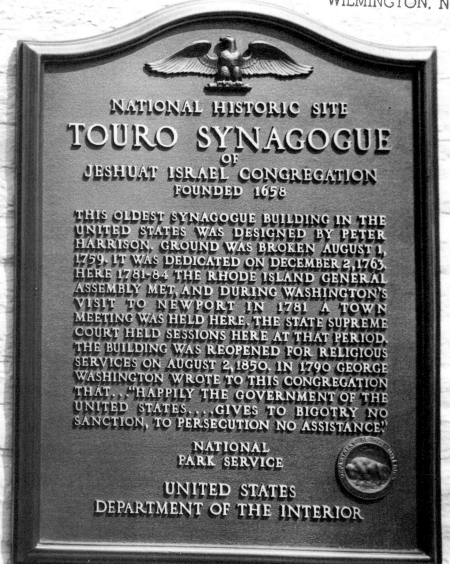

NATIONAL HISTORIC SITE

TOURO SYNAGOGUE

OF
JESHUAT ISRAEL CONGREGATION
FOUNDED 1658

THIS OLDEST SYNAGOGUE BUILDING IN THE UNITED STATES WAS DESIGNED BY PETER HARRISON. GROUND WAS BROKEN AUGUST 1, 1759. IT WAS DEDICATED ON DECEMBER 2, 1763. HERE 1781-84 THE RHODE ISLAND GENERAL ASSEMBLY MET, AND DURING WASHINGTON'S VISIT TO NEWPORT IN 1781 A TOWN MEETING WAS HELD HERE. THE STATE SUPREME COURT HELD SESSIONS HERE AT THAT PERIOD. THE BUILDING WAS REOPENED FOR RELIGIOUS SERVICES ON AUGUST 2, 1850. IN 1790 GEORGE WASHINGTON WROTE TO THIS CONGREGATION THAT..."HAPPILY THE GOVERNMENT OF THE UNITED STATES....GIVES TO BIGOTRY NO SANCTION, TO PERSECUTION NO ASSISTANCE"

NATIONAL
PARK SERVICE

UNITED STATES
DEPARTMENT OF THE INTERIOR

TO BIGOTRY NO SANCTION

The Story of the Oldest Synagogue in America

LEONARD EVERETT FISHER

HOLIDAY HOUSE / NEW YORK

Acknowledgments

I would like to thank B. Schlessinger Ross, Executive Director of The Friends of Touro Synagogue, Newport, Rhode Island, for her courteous and invaluable assistance. Also, my thanks to Rabbi Mordecai Eskowitz of the Touro Synagogue congregation for his enlightening historical perspectives; to Rabbi Robert J. Orkand of Temple Israel, Westport, Connecticut, for clarifying particular Judaic symbolism; and to Stanley Mark for his special assistance.

Mr. Fisher would like to thank the following persons and organizations for granting permission to use their photographs and artwork: Beth Hatefusoth, the Nahum Goldmann Museum of the Jewish Diaspora, Tel Aviv, page 19; Cabildo Catedral de Lleida, Spain, page 15; John T. Hopf © John T. Hopf Photography, half-title, pages 29, 39, 41, 42-43, 44, 45, 46, 47, 52-53, 56, 58, 63; Library of Congress, Prints & Photographs Division, HABS No. RI-278 (sheet 4 of 27), pages 36-37; Library of Congress, Prints & Photographs Division, HABS No. RI-278 (HABS RI 3-NEWP, 29-7), page 40; Library of Congress, Prints & Photographs Division, HABS No. RI-278 (HABS RI 3-NEWP, 29-10), page 48; Library of Congress, Prints & Photographs Division, HABS No. RI-278 (HABS RI 3-NEWP, 29 ⁸⁻¹), page 55; National Gallery of Art, Andrew W. Mellon Collection © 1998 Board of Trustees, page 6; New York Historical Society, page 25; Newport Historical Society, pages 30, 33; Peabody Essex Museum, page 57; Rhode Island Historial Society Negative Number Rhi (x3)19, page 26; Nina Woldin, page 12.

Mr. Fisher took the photographs for the jacket cover, frontis, and page 10.

Library of Congress Cataloging-in-Publication Data
Fisher, Leonard Everett.
To bigotry, no sanction: the story of the oldest synagogue in America/Leonard Everett Fisher.—1st ed.
p.   cm.
Includes bibliographical references and index.
Summary: The history of the oldest Jewish house of worship in the
United States, the Touro Synagogue, which was built in Newport,
Rhode Island, between 1759 and 1763.
ISBN 0-8234-1401-9
1. Touro Synagogue (Newport, R. I.)—History—Juvenile literature.
2. Jews—Rhode Island—Newport—History—Juvenile literature.
3. Sephardim—History—Juvenile literature. 4. Newport (R. I.)—
Ethnic relations—Juvenile literature. [1. Touro Synagogue
(Newport, R. I.) 2. Jews—Rhode Island—Newport. 3. Sephardim—
History. 4. Newport (R. I.)—Ethnic relations.] I. Title.
BM225. N572T64   1998   98-12834   CIP   AC
296'.09745'7—dc21

To Stanley & Joan Adler Mark

———————————————————————————

To the President of the United States of America

Sir:

Permit the children of the Stock of Abraham to approach you with the most cordial affection and esteem for your person & merits — and to join with our fellow citizens in welcoming you to NewPort.

With pleasure we reflect on those days — those days of difficulty, & danger, when the God of Israel, who delivered David from the peril of the sword — shielded Your head in the day of battle: — and we rejoice to think, that the same Spirit, who rested in the Bosom of the greatly beloved Daniel enabling him to preside over the Provinces of the Babylonish Empire, rests and ever will rest, upon you to discharge the arduous duties of Chief Magistrate in these States.

Deprived as we heretofore have been on the invaluable rights of free Citizens, we now with a deep sense of gratitude to the Almighty disposer of all events behold a Government, erected by the Majesty of the People — a Government, which to bigotry gives no sanction, to persecution no assistance — but generously affording to all Liberty of conscience, and immunities of Citizenship — deeming every one, of whatever Nation, tongue, or language equal parts of the great government machine; — This so ample and extensive Federal Union whose basis is Philanthropy, Mutual confidence and Public Virtue, we cannot but acknowledge to be the work of the Great God, who ruleth in the Armies of Heaven, and among the inhabitants of the Earth, doing whatever seemeth him good.

For all these Blessings of civil and religious liberty which we enjoy under an equal benign administration, we desire to send up our thanks to the Ancient of Days, the great preserver of Men — beseeching him, that the Angel who conducted our forefathers through the wilderness into the promised Land, may graciously conduct you through all the difficulties and dangers of this mortal life; — And, when, like Joshua full of days and full of honour, you are gathered to your Fathers, may you be admitted into the Heavenly Paradise to partake of the water of life and the tree of immortality.

Done and Signed by the order of the Hebrew Congregation in NewPort, Rhode Island August 17th 1790.

Moses Seixas, Warden

George Washington (Vaughn Portrait), 1795, oil on canvas by Gilbert Stuart

To the Hebrew Congregation in Newport, Rhode Island.

Gentlemen.

While I receive with much satisfaction, your Address replete with expressions of affection and esteem; I rejoice in the opportunity of assuring you, that I shall always retain a grateful remembrance of the cordial welcome I experienced in my visit to Newport, from all classes of Citizens.

The reflection on the days of difficulty and danger which are past is rendered the more sweet, from a consciousness that they are succeeded by days of uncommon prosperity and security. If we have wisdom to make the best use of the advantages with which we are now favored, we cannot fail, under the just administration of a good government, to become a great and a happy people.

The citizens of the United States of America have a right to applaud themselves for having given to mankind examples of an enlarged and liberal policy: a policy worthy of imitation. All possess alike liberty of conscience and immunities of citizenship. It is now no more that toleration is spoken of, as if it was by the indulgence of one class of people, that another enjoyed the exercise of their inherent natural rights. For happily the Government of the United States, which gives to bigotry no sanction, to persecution no assistance requires only that they who live under its protection should demean themselves as good citizens, in giving it on all occasions their effectual support.

It would be inconsistent with the frankness of my character not to avow that I am pleased with your favorable opinion of my administration, and fervent wishes for my felicity. May the Children of the stock of Abraham, who dwell in this land, continue to merit and enjoy the good will of the other Inhabitants; while every one shall sit in safety under his own vine and figtree, and there shall be none to make him afraid. May the father of all mercies scatter light and not darkness in our paths, and make us all in our several vocations useful here, and in his own due time and way everlastingly happy.

G. Washington

[August 21, 1790]

To Bigotry No Sanction

FOREWORD

The strains of the United States Navy Band floated over the oldest Jewish house of worship in the country, Touro Synagogue in Newport, Rhode Island. It was Sunday, August 19, 1990, the final day of the two-hundredth anniversary celebration of an exchange of letters between a synagogue official, Moses Seixas, and President George Washington. The key phrase in both, " . . . to bigotry no sanction, to persecution no assistance," was as remarkable in its aim as it was in its literary style.

The building of the Touro Synagogue between 1759 and 1763—in a soon-to-be independent United States of America—remains a bright chapter in a dark saga of religious persecution. The cruelty of this persecution would percolate into the nineteenth century and finally culminate in the Holocaust of the twentieth century.

The Touro Synagogue is a living symbol of America's refusal to travel the road of bigotry and persecution. As George Washington, quoting the Bible, wrote in his response to Moses Seixas's request for citizenship for the Jews in America:

Every one shall sit in safety . . . and there shall be none to make him afraid.

The Jews had arrived in Spain and other parts of western Europe immediately following the destruction of Jerusalem and its Temple by Rome. In A.D. 70, Spain, then a Roman province called Hispania, accepted Jews as slaves and noncitizens. They were granted full Roman citizenship in A.D. 212.

In A.D. 711, Muslim Berber tribesmen from Morocco—Moors—completed their conquest of the largely Christian Spanish peninsula. Only Portugal and the northern provinces of Castile, Aragon, and Navarre remained in Christian hands.

Jews continued to live in Spain after the Moors' conquest. The great caliph Hakam II, who ruled from 961 to 976 and was renowned for his support of the arts and sciences, left the affairs of state to his trusted prime minister, a Jew named Hasdai ibn Shaprut. Hakam constructed graceful mosques, schools, and centers of learning such as the renowned University of Córdoba. He built hospitals, provided asylums for the poor, and supported the work of poets, artists, philosophers, scientists, and mathematicians. Spain flourished.

Later, the Córdoba-born physician, Moses ben Maimon (1135–1204), also known as Maimonides, became a towering intellectual figure whose religious and secular writings were as respected among Christians and Muslims as they were among Jews.

In Córdoba, Christian, Jewish, and Moorish craftsmen, living, studying, and working together, tooled leather that became known the world over. They invented eyeglasses, built exceptional timepieces, and wove fine carpets and silk textiles, which were shipped to buyers in Europe, Africa, and Asia.

The Jews of Spain were comfortable in their Moorish surroundings. Their language, songs, and dress were more Moorish than Christian in style. One could hardly tell the difference between Moor and Jew.

Maimonides, also called Rambam, line drawing by Nina Woldin

In 1229, the Roman Catholic Church established the Holy Office of the Inquisition. Its purpose was to rout out all those who did not believe as the church wished them to believe. Jews, Muslims, scientists, artists, writers—all those who dared to be different—could be accused of heresy, a crime against both church and state.

The Spanish Inquisition began in 1480, following the marriage of King Ferdinand of Aragon and Queen Isabella of Castille in 1479. Non-Catholics were tormented and forced to convert to Catholicism or be executed for their beliefs.

The Catholic Church dominated Europe in 1492. Ferdinand and Isabella moved to include a united Spain in the family of Christian states. There would be no room for nonbelievers— Muslim and Jew alike.

On January 2, 1492, the Catholic army of King Ferdinand and Queen Isabella overpowered the Moors at Granada, the last Muslim stronghold in Spain. This victory brought to an end an enlightened Islamic culture in Spain. Religious liberty, granted by the Muslims to all people, ended. Islam would no longer be tolerated. The caliph, Boabdil, surrendered and rode off to a humiliating exile in Morocco. As Boabdil took a last tearful look at what he had given up, his mother, Sultana Ayxa, was said to have remarked, "You do well to weep as a woman over what you could not defend as a man."

Sharing the fate of the Moors were some 150,000 Jews, whose Spanish beginnings went back more than a thousand years— before the existence of any Muslim or Christian settlement there. They were all that were left of Spain's once flourishing Jewish population of 400,000. Some 250,000 Jews had been either massacred in the Christian outposts of the Spanish peninsula, become Christians, melted into the Spanish population, or moved elsewhere in Europe or North Africa.

King Ferdinand and Queen Isabella, Spanish tapestry

De Torres did this on their first encounter with the people of the New World. They had no idea what he was saying.

Another Spanish Jew, Abraham Zacuto, a professor of mathematics and cartography at the University of Salamanca, provided Columbus with the up-to-date charts and navigational tables he needed for his adventure into the unknown seas. Zacuto fled to Portugal, where, favored by King John II, he created the navigation charts that enabled Portuguese sailors, such as Vasco da Gama, to roam the world's oceans.

Columbus's trip, financed by Isabella and Ferdinand, was made possible, in part, by the Crown's confiscation of Jewish properties. On the day Columbus planned to leave—August 2—the Gulf of Cádiz was so congested with the Jewish Expulsion that he could not get underway on the outgoing tide. He had to wait to sail the next day.

The Jews had few places to go. The German states had been continuously murdering Jews along the Rhine River since 1096; England had expelled them in 1290; France in 1392. The rest of Europe was unwelcoming. Only North Africa, the Netherlands, Italy, and Turkey offered safe havens. Some Jews, such as Abraham Zacuto, escaped to Portugal and were safe as long as King John II sat on the throne. Unlike the Jews, the Moors had but to cross the Mediterranean Sea and settle on Islamic territory in North Africa to find refuge.

King John II of Portugal died in 1495. He was succeeded by his cousin and brother-in-law Manuel I. The Jews in Portugal would know no peace under the new king.

Manuel wanted to marry the daughter of Isabella and Ferdinand. To make himself acceptable to the powerful Spanish rulers, he issued an edict on Christmas Day, December 25, 1496, requiring Jews in Portugal to either convert to Catholicism or leave the country in ten months, by October 1497.

Some Jews were lucky enough to escape the country by sea. By the end of October 1497, twenty thousand hapless Jews jammed Lisbon's harbor, unable to go anywhere. There were no ships for them. Manuel imprisoned those who did not commit suicide, forcibly baptizing them. Only a handful escaped. Among them was a Marrano, Fernando de Loronha.

Manuel made a deal with de Loronha. In 1502, as Spain's Muslims sailed across the Mediterranean toward a new life in North Africa, Manuel allowed de Loronha and five shiploads of desperate Jews to flee the Inquisition and settle the Brazilian coast of South America. They were to explore and fortify this area for the Portuguese Crown. They would be the first Jewish settlers in the New World.

Among the passengers to make the trip was Amerigo Vespucci, an Italian shipfitter, astronomer, and explorer, one of several Christians in the group. Returning from this trip, Vespucci wrote that this land was not India or the islands of the Indies, as previously thought, but a new continent. He would be proven right. The new continents, North and South America, would be named for him.

No one in Spain, Portugal, or Hispanic America of the 1500s could predict that the colonization of the Americas would offer a haven for the unwanted of the world.

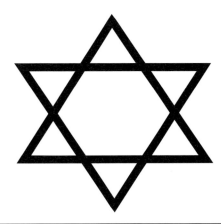

*T*he bulk of the expelled Spanish Jews moved eastward toward the tolerant Ottoman Empire, a vast land of Muslim Turks extending from eastern Europe into western Asia and eastern Africa. The Turks offered religious liberty to all of the empire's inhabitants, including Jews.

A small numbers of Jews, hiding their identities, crossed the Atlantic Ocean as early as 1521, seeking permanent havens in the newly conquered territories, despite Spanish edicts prohibiting Jewish settlement in the Americas. The Spanish Inquisition relentlessly pursued those stateless Jews who managed to establish themselves in the West Indies and Central and South America, where Spanish soldier-adventurers—conquistadores—among them Conversos, had conquered the native populations and claimed the Americas for the Spanish throne. Betrayed by informers, hidden Jews and Conversos in Mexico, Peru, and elsewhere were burned alive at the stake as the subdued Aztecs, Mayans, or Incas looked on in terror.

Among the most prominent of these adventurers was a Portuguese-born Spanish conquistador of secret Jewish extraction, Don Luis Carvajals. In 1579, King Phillip II of Spain, unaware of Don Carvajals's background, appointed him governor of the New Kingdom of León, a Spanish land grant in northern Mexico, then called New Spain. Don Luis brought with him a number of families, most of whom were secret Jews. These included his brother-in-law, Don Francisco Rodriguez de Matos, a rabbi, and Don Francisco's oldest son, Luis, a Catholic priest, but a secret Jew, and other members of his immediate family.

When the Holy Office of the Inquisition, now operating in Mexico City, discovered that Don Luis Carvajals, his family, and other colonizers were truly Jews who were Christian in name only, they began to destroy them all systematically. The first to be arrested

Spanish horsemen depicted in a Navajo Indian pictograph panel, Canyon del Muerto, Canyon de Chelly National Monument, Arizona.

was the governor himself, Don Luis, who was a first- or second-generation Converso and claimed never to have known about his Jewish heritage. Don Luis died in prison in 1590. Between 1596 and 1649, many of Don Luis's relatives and associates were tried in Mexico City, convicted of being secret Jews, and burned at the stake. Those who remained escaped northwestward into the uncharted lands of what is today's American Southwest.

Jews in Brazil and on the island of Barbados in the West Indies fared a little better. Unmolested for about 150 years, they had become successful sugar and tobacco planters. They exported their products to relatives and friends who had resettled in North Africa, Italy, Holland, and Turkey in return for tools, books, textiles, furniture, and other hard goods.

In 1654, the Brazilian Jews were hunted down by agents of the Portuguese Inquisition, despite the contract made earlier between King Manuel and Fernando de Loronha. Twenty-three of them fled Recife and found their way to the Dutch colony of New Amsterdam—present-day New York City. Peter Stuyvesant, the governor, protested their arrival to the colony's proprietors, the Dutch West India Company in Amsterdam. But given the tradition of Dutch welcome of dispossessed Jews following their expulsion from Spain, the Dutch West India Company ruled that Governor Stuyvesant, who himself was an officer in the company, had to accept them. He did so grudgingly.

Undaunted and unmolested, these Brazilian Jews remained as contributing citizens of the colony, forging a trading business in sugar with their friends in Barbados. Here, in New Amsterdam, they established the first Jewish congregation in America, Shearith Israel—"Remnant of Israel."

Peter Stuyvesant, portrait by unidentified artist

A KEY TO THE NATIVE LANGUAGE OF
AMERICA BY ROGER WILLIAMS

BLOODY TENET

Religious disputes were having their effect in the colonies of New England during this same period. In 1636, Roger Williams, an English minister, had been driven out of the Massachusetts Bay Colony by an intolerant Puritan clergy. The clergy objected to his belief in freedom of religion and to his stand that the spiritual requirements of the Church of England should be separated from the civil government of England. These ideas, religious freedom and the separation of church and state, would become cornerstones in the establishment not only of the Rhode Island Colony, where Williams became president in 1654, but also of a new American nation founded more than a century later.

Three years following Roger Williams's expulsion from the Massachusetts Bay Colony, Nicholas Easton, William Coddington, and John Clarke also fled Massachusetts for religious reasons. They founded Newport as a "lively experiment."

A few years later, when Puritan Oliver Cromwell defeated Charles I and had him beheaded, Roger Williams returned to England to fight for his charter and ideals, none of which were acceptable to the English republic, which was now called Protectorate, and ruled by Cromwell as a dictator.

However, in 1644, Cromwell granted Williams the charter he sought that empowered the Providence Plantations to call themselves "Rhode Island" and created a place in which civil government was separate from spiritual matters. The charter allowed the Rhode Island colonists to govern themselves "conformable to the laws of England, so far as the nature and constitution of the place will admit."

Williams expressed pleasure in achieving the separation of church and state when he wrote in 1647, "all men may walk as their consciences persuade them, everyone in the name of his God."

Roger Williams, portrait by F. Halpin, 1847, engraving

*I*n 1658, a handful of Jews from the island of Curaçao in the Dutch West Indies, led by Moses Pacheco and Mordecai Campanall, arrived in the small coastal town of Newport. They would not be the only group to seek religious liberty in Newport. The Society of Friends, or Quakers, having been expelled from New Amsterdam by the Dutch in 1657, also appeared in Newport. Eventually, Newport would become a refuge for unhappy Baptists—Roger Williams himself would become a Baptist—Congregationalists, Presbyterians, Episcopalians, Anglicans, Moravians, Huguenots (French Protestants), Catholics, and others.

For their part, the Newport Jews could hardly believe what had befallen them. No one hunted them down. No one objected to their presence in Newport or anywhere else in Rhode Island. No one complained about their ancient religious beliefs and practices. They were permitted to carry on their lives and livelihoods according to their own desires. The only thing they could not do was vote on the colony's affairs. But this did not seem as important to them as putting their heritage together again in a welcoming land where they could be useful and upstanding citizens.

All this would be confirmed by the General Assembly of the Colony of Rhode Island and Providence Plantations, which addressed a petition presented on June 24, 1684, by Newport Jews who worried over their status as outsiders. The General Assembly declared: "[Jews] may expect as good protection here, as any stranger residing amongst us in his Majesty's Colony ought to have, being obedient to his Majesty's laws . . ."

All too aware of their past, the Jews of Newport, still few in number, were not all that certain of their welcome in a town that offered them protection but called them strangers. For example,

they had no consecrated place in which to bury their dead. The lack of such a place was a cause of great anxiety among them. They needed a burial place to give them a feeling of permanency. Finally, by 1677, they were able to purchase the land and consecrate it as a burial ground with little difficulty. Here they could bury their dead according to the ancient traditions of their ancestors.

They did not have a synagogue, either, in which they could pray, around which they could rally, and where their children could be schooled in their faith. Instead, their services and special holiday observances were held in various homes.

The Jewish presence in Newport waxed and waned for a hundred years. Yet they managed to form a congregation—although one without a name. Some came and left. Some came and stayed. No one returned to South America. In fact, by 1700, there were no Jews left in South America—at least none who openly practiced or admitted their Jewish faith. The congregation stood.

Above: The Eternal Light, Touro Synagogue

In 1700, one of the most imposing of the several hundred buildings in Newport was the Great Meeting House of the Quakers. And at that juncture, Newport was well on its way to becoming a maritime commercial rival of Boston, New York, and Philadelphia. Moreover, thirty years into the new century—1730—Newport had become a very enlightened society, home to philosophers like George Berkeley; printers like Benjamin Franklin's older brother, James; and artists like John Smibert and later, Gilbert Stuart, who earned his living painting George Washington's portrait.

True, the early farmers of Newport had built a wealthy, agriculturally based society. The seal of the Town of Newport, created in 1696, shows a sheep, not a ship, as the core of its design. Still, given her fine harbor, Newport's chief source of wealth was the sea. A great number of people living and working in Newport were involved with ships and the sea. They either built the ships, sailed them, owned them, supplied them, or filled them with all manner of goods and raw materials, including African slaves.

By midcentury, Quakers who had come from New York, England, and Barbados, and Jews who had come from Curaçao, Barbados, Jamaica, England, Amsterdam, and central and eastern Europe, had left behind many friendly connections that developed into substantial customers for Newport's seafaring merchants. Among these merchant-shippers were Abraham Redwood, a Quaker, and Aaron Lopez, a Jew who had once been a Catholic in Portugal and assumed the name Duarte Lopez. He returned to his Jewish roots in Newport and was renamed Aaron. The industry of both Redwood and Lopez made Newport a center of commerce and intellect, and themselves the wealthiest and most powerful men in Newport. Aaron Lopez enjoyed the close friendship of Ezra Stiles, a New Haven, Connecticut, theologian, who was appointed Newport's Congregational minister in 1755. Dr. Stiles described

---

Harrison had come from York, England, twenty years before, bringing with him a large architectural library. Included among these books were works by Andrea Palladio, the Italian architect whose style, rooted in classical Greece and Rome, influenced Harrison's own plans, as well as the style of early federal buildings in the United States.

Until Harrison came along, great houses and public buildings in colonial America were the work of "housewrights" and "masterbuilders" such as Newport's Richard Munday, who copied ideas and building methods from a variety of architectural books published in England. But Harrison's understanding of architectural principles, his knowledge of historical styles and construction, was profound. He was the first in America to express the new classical style of Palladio in its less monumental terms. Peter Harrison was something more than a "masterbuilder." He was an architect—America's first.

In 1748, Harrison, then thirty-two years old, had already designed the Redwood Library. But now, in 1759, Harrison turned his attention to the synagogue. There is no record of any request by Harrison for payment, or any record that such payment had ever been made to him for designing the synagogue.

As Harrison polished his design, the congregation quickly realized that their funds would not be sufficient to complete the building. They dispatched letters pleading for financial help. On March 21, 1759, they wrote to Congregation Shearith Israel of New York:

We have lately purchased a suitable lot of land, whereon we design to build a Synagogue; & for furthering our said intentions, we have likewise by subscription raised a small fund, wherewith to begin, and carry on the work and which in due time, we hope to see fully compleated. At present finding our abilities not equal to our wishes, for finishing the work we crave the assistance of the several Congregations in America.

Help was quickly forthcoming not only from New York, but from London and the West Indies. Ground was broken on August 1, 1759, followed by the laying of a foundation and cornerstone. The work progressed in fits and starts over the next four years as funds ran out and funds were received. One London congregation, Bevis Marks, apologized for their inability to provide any money at all: "We praise you very much but at the present time it would not be convenient for us, nor are we able to comply with your request. May God be the one who assists all."

Instead, Bevis Marks shipped across the Atlantic Ocean two alms boxes for the collection of money. These alms boxes were eventually attached to two columns inside the completed synagogue at its entrance. They are there to this day.

As the walls of the building—walls of brick imported from London—rose and gave it shape, Isaac Touro found himself deep in religious conversations with Ezra Stiles. For his own enlightenment, Stiles gently prodded Touro to reveal all he knew regarding Judaism, recording his observations and thoughts along the way from a Christian perspective. In some way, Stiles likened the great English North American emigration to the struggle of the ancient Hebrews of the Old Testament to reach Jerusalem, the "Promised Land." Touro was only too willing to unveil all of his considerable knowledge while listening and responding to Stiles's educated interpretations and questions. Stiles absorbed it all, including the Hebrew language, in which he became fluent.

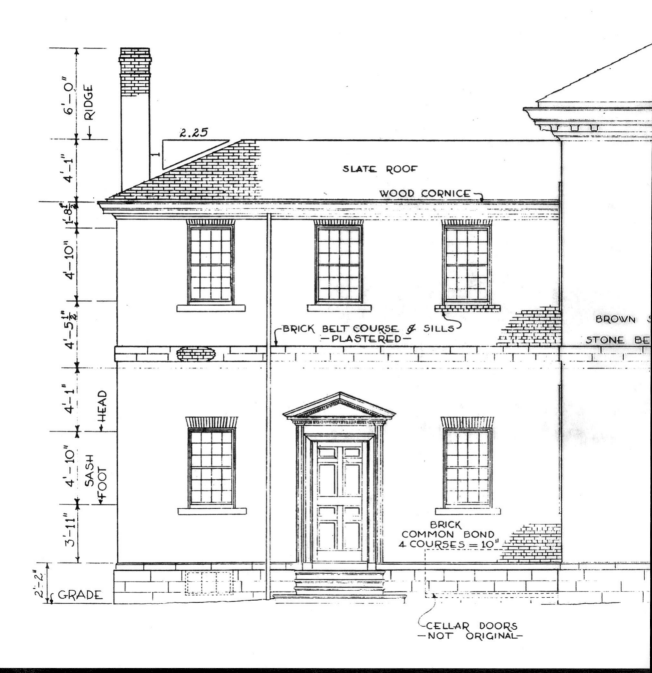

SLATE ROOF

WOOD CORNICE

BRICK BELT COURSE & SILLS
—PLASTERED—

BROWN S

STONE BE

RIDGE

6'-0"

4'-1"

1'-8½"

4'-10"

4'-5½"

2.25

4'-1" — HEAD

4'-10" SASH FOOT

3'-11"

2'-2" — GRADE

BRICK
COMMON BOND
4 COURSES = 10"

CELLAR DOORS
—NOT ORIGINAL—

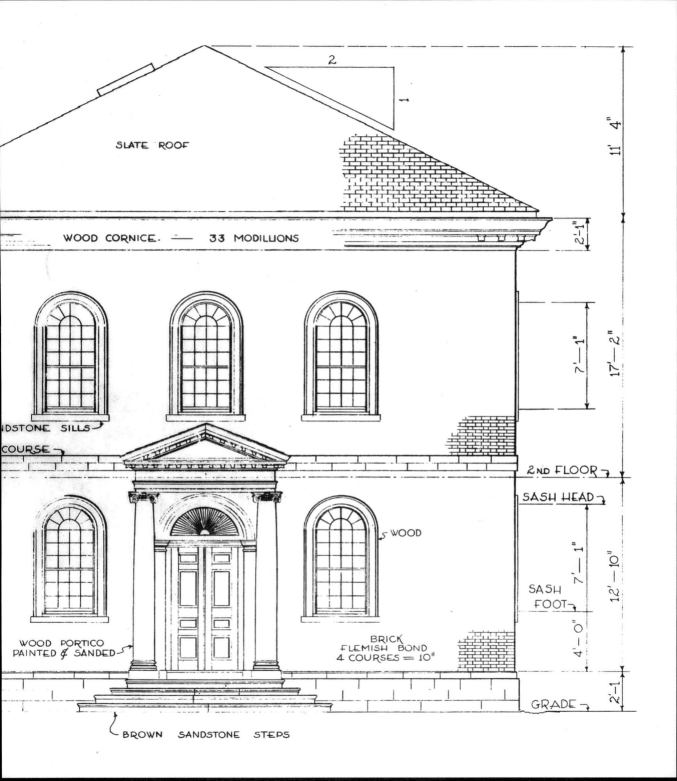

SLATE ROOF

2

1

11' 4"

WOOD CORNICE. —— 33 MODILLIONS

2'-1"

NDSTONE SILLS

COURSE

7'-1"

17'—2"

2ND FLOOR

SASH HEAD

WOOD

12'—10"

SASH
FOOT

7'—1"

WOOD PORTICO
PAINTED & SANDED

BRICK
FLEMISH BOND
4 COURSES = 10"

4'-0"

GRADE

2'-1

BROWN SANDSTONE STEPS

Typical of Stiles's open mind and inexhaustible enthusiasm were his meetings with Chaim Isaac Carigal, a rabbi from the city of Hebron in the Holy Land, the burial site of Abraham, the founder of Judaism. Stiles described Rabbi Carigal as "learned and truly modest." Carigal traveled the world, visiting Jewish congregations. He came to Newport in 1772 and stayed a year. During that time he gave sermons in Spanish while Stiles engaged him in numerous theological discussions. Stiles wrote it all down in a diary. This entry of June 14, 1773, shows the essence of their meetings:

> I turned him to the strong expression in his letter to me, "Your love has made such an indelible impression upon the inmost thoughts and affections of my heart that volumes are not sufficient to write the thousandth part of the eternal love wherewith I love thee"—and asked him how he could use so strong an expression of friendship. He . . . said he wished well to others . . . he loved all mankind, and turned me to Leviticus XIX, 18—Thou shalt love thy neighbor as thyself.

Finally, after four years of work, the two-story synagogue, still without a name, stood completed. Quietly graceful in its simple exterior, it was immediately marked as an extraordinary example of religious feeling cloaked in a Georgian style. The synagogue's symmetry was broken only by a small wing on the north side, its school. The quietness of the building's exterior, its gentleness, belied the tormented history of its congregants, resolute in their beliefs. What Peter Harrison caught was a calmness that expressed an end to their search for freedom and peace of mind.

Peter Harrison, portrait

The sense of peace that the building's exterior communicated gave way to a somewhat more exuberant interior. The interior seemed more spacious and soaring than it actually was. Its warm gray woodwork and whitewashed walls reflected an American place. Yet, its features also mirrored the religious services as conducted in the Sephardic tradition, the tradition of Spanish and Portuguese Jews, who formed the heart of the congregation. The few Jewish congregants from Poland and Russia, who formerly worshiped in the Ashkenazic or eastern European tradition, now prayed in the same manner as their Sephardic brethren.

Men worshiped on the main sanctuary floor, while women worshiped in the upstairs galleries that encircled the sanctuary on three sides. These galleries were supported by twelve Ionic columns, representing the twelve biblical tribes of Israel. Another twelve columns in the Corinthian style, again representing the twelve tribes of biblical Israel, rose from the upstairs galleries to the ceiling of the synagogue. The same symbolism applied to the

Left: Touro Synagogue   *Above:* Jacob Pollack Chandelier, Touro Synagogue
Pages 42-43: Interior of Touro Synagogue

large twelve-branch candelabras that were suspended from the ceiling of the building.

On December 2, 1763, Isaac Touro was appointed rabbi of the congregation, a post he was to hold for twenty years until his death on December 3, 1783. On the day of his appointment, Dr. Touro stood on the raised platform, or *bimah,* in the center of the sanctuary, facing east toward the holy city of Jerusalem, surrounded by a sea of distinguished Christians and Jews. Most stood for the lack of chairs. At the eastern end of the room was the Holy Ark, built to contain Torah scrolls, and the pulpit for sermons. A single pew along the north wall was reserved for the most honored dignitaries. On this solemn occasion, Isaac Touro dedicated the synagogue's presence for all time.

While the wide floorboards of the synagogue were bare, Isaac Touro stood on a carpet that covered a trapdoor and ladder that led to a room hidden below the bimah. There was no tunnel or door leading from any part of it to somewhere else. Other than perhaps a chair or two, there was no furniture to be found in it.

Above: Hanukkah Candelabra, Touro Synagogue
Right: Entrance to Underground Passage, Touro Synagogue

According to Sephardic tradition, Spanish and Portuguese Jews kept such secret rooms in their synagogues to hide from the agents of the Inquisition. The Jews of Newport, living in a land without the cruelty of an inquisition, did not need such a place. They included it to remind them of their experience. Perhaps, too, knowing deep in their hearts that the future was never certain for them, even in Rhode Island, they viewed such a room as a hiding place.

Newport's newspaper, *The Newport Mercury*, reported the historic dedication as having "a handsome Assembly of People, in an Edifice the most perfect of the Temple kind perhaps in America." It went on to say of the dedicatory service: "[It] could not but raise in the Mind a faint Idea of the Majesty & Grandeur of the Ancient Jewish Worship mentioned in Scripture."

By June 1764, Newport's Jewish congregation had deposited in the Holy Ark three Torah scrolls on which the writings of Moses were inscribed. One of these scrolls, which came from Amsterdam, was more than two hundred years old at the time. This same scroll is still in place in the synagogue's Holy Ark.

Three years following the dedication, the congregation was no longer without a name. Having built their synagogue, the Newport congregation took the name Yeshuat Israel—"Salvation of Israel."

But protest over England's treatment of her colonies was in the air everywhere. On the eve of revolution there were about three million people in the colonies of which some three thousand were Jews scattered from Boston, Massachusetts, to Savannah, Georgia.

The Revolutionary War took its toll on Newport. The British occupied the city between 1776 and 1779, and this occupation smothered the life of the city.

Newport's Jews were sympathetic to the patriot cause. Isaac Touro, Moses Hays, Meyer Pollack, and Isaac Hart, all members of the synagogue, refused to sign a loyalty oath that the British imposed upon Newport. They argued that they were not British subjects, because they were not granted citizenship, being members of the Society of Israelites. The four were arrested, charged under the Suspected Persons Act, and tried. They were acquitted, having proved that as noncitizens, they could not be disloyal to the Crown.

About half of Newport's eleven thousand people, Christian and Jew alike, supported the American cause and left Newport during this time. There was hardly anyone left to attend any kind of church or synagogue service. Ezra Stiles and most of his followers fled to Massachusetts. Isaac Touro and most of his followers fled to New York or Boston. The synagogue closed. Rabbi Touro ended up on the island of Jamaica, where he died in 1783.

Interior of Touro Synagogue

He was forty-six years old. At his death he was still the spiritual leader of the now defunct Congregation Yeshuat Israel of Newport, Rhode Island.

When the British withdrew, French troops under General Jean de Rochambeau moved in. They found a nearly empty city with many of its buildings badly damaged and in need of repair. Some people returned and tried to restore Newport to its prewar vitality, but to no avail.

The synagogue reopened for religious services in 1781, but few came. Since many of the city's ruined public buildings were of little use, the synagogue became the center of city and state civil and judicial activities. Between 1781 and 1784, the synagogue served as the meeting place of the Rhode Island General Assembly. Here, too, the Rhode Island Supreme Court sat in session and the Town of Newport held meetings. George Washington himself came to Newport in 1781 to meet with Rochambeau and plan the American southern campaign, which would end with the final British defeat at Yorktown, Virginia. That meeting was held at the synagogue.

Washington returned to Newport nine years later on a trip in support of the adoption of the Bill of Rights, the first ten amendments to the United States Constitution. The first eight amendments of the Bill of Rights protected the basic liberties of every American citizen—such as freedom of religion, speech, the press, and the right of assembly—not guaranteed by the Constitution itself when it became the law of the land in 1789. The last two amendments prohibited Congress from passing any laws that would violate the first eight.

It was during this visit that Washington was approached by Newport's few Jews. However free and unmolested they were, Jews in America still could not vote. And Jews though they were, they were still New Englanders and painfully aware of

Washington's 1775 description of New Englanders in general. Speaking as a southern gentleman, Washington had described northern farmers, homemakers, craftsmen, merchants, tradesmen, and seafarers as "exceedingly dirty and nasty people."

After the war Washington changed his mind somewhat when he grudgingly said of New Englanders, "I do not believe that any of the states produce better men or persons capable of making better soldiers."

Given the history of the Jewish people, Newport's Jews were concerned about their status in the new nation. With all this in mind, Moses Seixas phrased his letter to George Washington as sensitively as possible. Hoping for the best, Newport's Jewish community received more than they asked. Washington's echoing response—"For happily the Government of the United States, which gives to bigotry no sanction, to persecution no assistance"—went beyond a mere affirmation of the government's policy to protect the religious freedom of everyone in America. It was the tone of the letter that was so exceptional: warmly sincere, full of respect and friendship. The Jews of Newport and elsewhere were more secure in their American future than ever before.

In that same year, 1790, George Washington demonstrated the same sincerity and warmth in his response to a congratulatory letter from the Kahal Kadosh Beth Elohim (Holy Congregational House of God) of Charleston, South Carolina, then in the throes of planning its own synagogue. Joseph Levy, America's first Jewish military officer, was a member of the Charleston congregation. Another congregant, Francis Salvador, a delegate to the South Carolina Provincial Congress, was the first South Carolinian to die for America's cause in the Revolutionary War. To this Jewish congregation, George Washington wrote: "May the same temporal and eternal blessing which you implore for me, rest upon your Congregation."

Pages 52-53: Interior of Touro Synagogue

Despite that feeling of security, and despite the fanfare and celebrations that marked George Washington's historic 1790 visit to Newport, the city's fortunes, never having recovered from the Revolutionary War, continued to deteriorate. The brutal British occupation had left its mark. Newport's buildings, wharfs, and public places were still in ruins and fast crumbling. For the next thirty years, Newport's synagogue slid into the rot and ruin that was afflicting the rest of the city. Had it not been for Isaac Touro's two sons, Abraham Touro of Boston and Judah Touro of Boston and New Orleans, the synagogue would have decayed to the point of being demolished altogether.

Both brothers had amassed considerable fortunes in business enterprises. And both brothers, along with their sister, Rebecca, retained a deep attachment to Newport's synagogue and to the Jewish burial ground there. The Touro brothers were well aware of the historic significance of the synagogue as it related not only to early Jewish presence in America, but also as the place in which their father, Isaac, served the Jewish population at the height of its glory. Their interest took on special meaning now that there was not a single Jew left in Newport.

Abraham died in 1822. He left money at his death for the restoration and preservation of the synagogue. This money was called the Touro Jewish Synagogue Fund. Following the establishment of this fund, the synagogue became known as the Touro Synagogue. What made the bequest somewhat unusual was that never before in America had any money been bequeathed for preserving historic buildings.

Within a few years of Abraham's death, work began on the restoration of Touro Synagogue. The building was eventually returned to its former splendor. It remained closed, however, except for special occasions.

Judah Touro had left Boston for New Orleans in 1800. He died there in 1854. He was buried in Newport's Jewish cemetery where Aaron Lopez and Moses Seixas also rest. During his lifetime, Judah Touro contributed large sums of money to Catholic, Protestant, and Jewish charities. The contributions continued beyond his death. His obituary in the *Newport Daily News* said, in part: "His parents and relatives were of the Jewish faith and he adhered to the religion of his fathers through life, though he contributed liberal sums for many Christian enterprises."

Judah Touro's will established a fund to care for Newport's Jewish cemetery, to purchase some land nearby to be called Touro Park, to provide a salary for either a Touro Synagogue rabbi or a *chazzan*, a reader of the Torah, and to put up a fence around the cemetery and synagogue proper. The cemetery fence was installed in 1842. The synagogue fence appeared in 1843.

Abraham Touro, portrait by Gilbert Stuart

Isaac Touro, portrait by Gilbert Stuart

Judah Touro, portrait

*T*ouro Synagogue remained closed for regular worship until the waning years of the nineteenth century. In 1883, a number of Jews came to Newport from eastern Europe. They were part of the movement of millions of Jews to the United States who were fleeing the bloodletting and carnage following the assassination of Russia's tsar Alexander II in 1881.

Enough Jews came to Newport to reactivate the Yeshuat Israel Congregation—ten men were necessary to create a prayer service—and open Touro Synagogue. This they did in a perfectly preserved building, according to the Sephardic traditions of its former occupants, rather than the Ashkenazic traditions from which they came. The decision to worship in the Sephardic tradition was made, on one hand, out of respect for the original Spanish/Portuguese congregation, and its historic place in American life; and, on the other hand, out of respect for tradition itself and its continuation in this House of God.

The only change these Jews from eastern Europe made was in the spelling of the congregation's name. Instead of being called Yeshuat Israel, they were now called Jeshuat Israel. The small spelling change did not alter the Hebrew meaning, "Salvation of Israel." The entire enterprise was encouraged by New York's Shearith Israel, who held in trust the title to Touro Synagogue.

In 1946, in the aftermath of World War II and the Holocaust, the world began to assess the human carnage. Six million Jews had been tortured and murdered by the German Nazis. None of these Jews would ever know the religious liberty of America. And none of their oppressors seemed able to grasp the American ideal of religious liberty as stated in the First Amendment to the Constitution: "Congress shall make no law respecting an establishment of religion, or prohibiting the free exercise thereof . . ."

On March 5, 1946, to honor that cornerstone of American ideals, President Harry S. Truman designated Touro Synagogue as a National Historic Site, a symbol of religious liberty. He wrote:

The setting apart of this historic shrine as a national monument is symbolic of our tradition of freedom. I trust through long centuries to come that the spirit of good will and tolerance will ever dominate the hearts and minds of the American people.

In 1954, Touro Synagogue began a second restoration, which was completed in 1963. On September 15, 1963, President John Fitzgerald Kennedy wrote:

It [Touro] is not only the oldest Synagogue in America but also one of the oldest symbols of liberty. No better tradition exists than the history of the Touro Synagogue's great contribution to the goals of freedom and justice for all.

On September 15, 1968, another American president, Dwight David Eisenhower, came to Touro Synagogue and read George Washington's letter to the congregation. No other American president had experienced firsthand what had befallen Europe's Jews during World War II. As commander of the victorious Allied Forces in Europe, General Eisenhower had visited the prison camps and had seen the horror for himself. Prior to his visit, he wrote to Dr. Bernard C. Friedman, president of the Society of Friends of Touro Synagogue:

During his visit to Newport in 1790, Washington called for more than tolerance. He reminded your forebears of the natural rights and responsibilities of each citizen of our land. On these two pillars of democracy, united in faith of brothers under God, our country finds the foundation of its strength and the world finds continued hope for the peaceful progress of mankind.

It is a privilege to take part in this great tradition of Touro Synagogue and to reaffirm my basic belief in the first article of our Bill of Rights, America's freedom of worship.

Twenty-two years later, on Sunday, August 19, 1990, an honor guard of the Newport Artillery stood in full colonial uniform before Touro Synagogue. The sound of the United States Navy Band softened and drifted away. A distinguished audience had gathered to observe the two-hundredth anniversary of the Touro-Washington exchange of letters. Seventeen-year-old Joshua Seixas Fausty, a descendant of Moses Seixas, concluded the ceremonies by reading his ancestor's letter to George Washington.

And, when, like Joshua full of days and full of honour, you are gathered to your Fathers, may you be admitted into the Heavenly Paradise to partake of the water of life and the tree of immortality.

Touro Synagogue is a symbol of liberty, reminding the world of its ultimate responsibility to give bigotry no sanction and persecution no assistance.

BIBLIOGRAHY

Boorstin, Daniel. *The Discoverers.* New York: Random House, 1983.

Commager, H. S., and R. B. Morris. *The Spirit of '76.* New York: Harper & Row, 1967.

Dimont, Max I. *Jews, God and History.* New York: Simon & Schuster, 1962.

Durant, Will. *The Story of Civilization,* Vol. IV, *The Age of Faith.* New York: Simon & Schuster, 1950.

Fisher, Leonard Everett. *The Architects.* New York: Franklin Watts, 1970.

————. *The Silversmiths.* New York: Marshall Cavendish, 1996.

Hawke, David. *The Colonial Experience.* New York: Bobbs Merrill, 1966.

Irving, Washington. *The Alhambra.* New York: T. Y. Crowell, 1851.

Jefferys, C.P.B. *Newport, A Short History.* Newport: Newport Historical Society, 1992.

Kastein, Josef. *History and Destiny of the Jews.* New York: Viking, 1933.

Lewis, Rabbi Dr. Theodore. *History of Touro Synagogue.* Newport: Bulletin of the Newport Historical Society, Summer 1975. No. 159; vol. 48, part 3.

Notes of the Rhode Island Jewish Historical Association. Nov. 1990, Vol. 10, No. 4; Nov. 1991, Vol. 11, No. 1.

Rochlin, Harriet and Fred. *Pioneer Jews.* Boston: Houghton Mifflin, 1984.

Touro Synagogue. National Park Service, United States Department of the Interior/Society of Friends of Touro Synagogue National Historic Shrine, Inc., 1996.

Painting of the Ten Commandments, Touro Synagogue

Redwood, Abraham, 31-32, 34
Redwood Library and Atheneum, 32, **33**, 34
religious liberty, 11, 14, 23, 27, 28, 32, 47,
  50, 51, 59, 60, 61
religious persecution, 11, 20
  (*see also* Spanish Inquisition)
  in England, 20
  in France, 20
  in Germany, 20
  in the New World, 24, 27, 28, 50-51
  in Portugal, 20, 47
  in Rome, 13
Revolutionary War, 49-51, 54
Rhode Island Colony, 27, 28
  (*see also* Newport, Rhode Island)
Rhode Island General Assembly, 28, 50
Rhode Island Supreme Court, 50
Rochambeau, Jean de, 50
Roman Catholic Church, 14
  Alexander VI (pope), 16

Sabbath, 16
Salvador, Francis, 51
secret rooms (in synagogues), 44, **45**, 47
Seixas, Moses, 7, 8, 11, 51, 55, 61
Sephardic tradition, 41, 47, 59
Shearith Israel ("Remnant of Israel"), 24, 34-
  35, 59
Society of Friends (Quakers), 28, 31
Society of Friends of Touro Synagogue, 60
South America, 21, 23, 24, 29
  Jews settle in, 21
South Carolina, 51
Spain, 13, 47, 59 (*see also* Ferdinand and
  Isabella)
  Jews in, 13, 14, 16-17, 20-21, 41
Spanish Inquisition, 14, 16-17, 20-21, 23, 47
Stiles, Ezra, 31-32, 35, 38, 49
Stuyvesant, Peter, 24, **25**
Suspected Persons Act, 49

Torah, 44, **46**, **47**, 49, 55
Torquemada, Tomás de (inquisitor general),
  16-17
Touro, Abraham, 54, **56**
Touro, Isaac, 32, 35, 44, 49-50, 54, **57**
Touro, Judah, 54, 55, **58**
Touro, Rebecca, 54
Touro Jewish Synagogue Fund, 54
Touro Park, 55

Touro Synagogue, 11, 54
  building of, 32-38
  as civil meeting place, 50
  closing of, 49, 54, 59
  dedication of, 44, 47, 49
  designing of, 32, 34, **36-37**
  exterior of, 38, **40**, 41
  first congregation, 29, 32, 49
  interior of, **10**, **30**, 35, 41, **41**, **42-43**, 44,
    44-45, **48**, **52-53**,
  naming of, 38, 49, 54, 59
  as National Historic Site, 60
  preservation of, 54
  raising money for, 34-35
  reopening of, 50, 59
  second restoration of, 60

trade, Jewish establishment of, 24, 31
  in Brazil, 24
  in Newport, Rhode Island, 31
  in Spain, 13
Truman, Harry S., 60
Turkey, 20, 24
Turks, 23

University of Córdoba, 13

Vespucci, Amerigo, 21

Washington, George, **6**, 7, 8, 11, 50-51, 54,
  60, 61
West Indies, 17, 21, 24, 28, 35
Williams, Roger, **26**, 27, 28
World War II, 59, 60

Yeshuat Israel ("Salvation of Israel"),
  49-50, 59

Zacuto, Abraham, 20

ML